THE CAT
AND
THE COOK

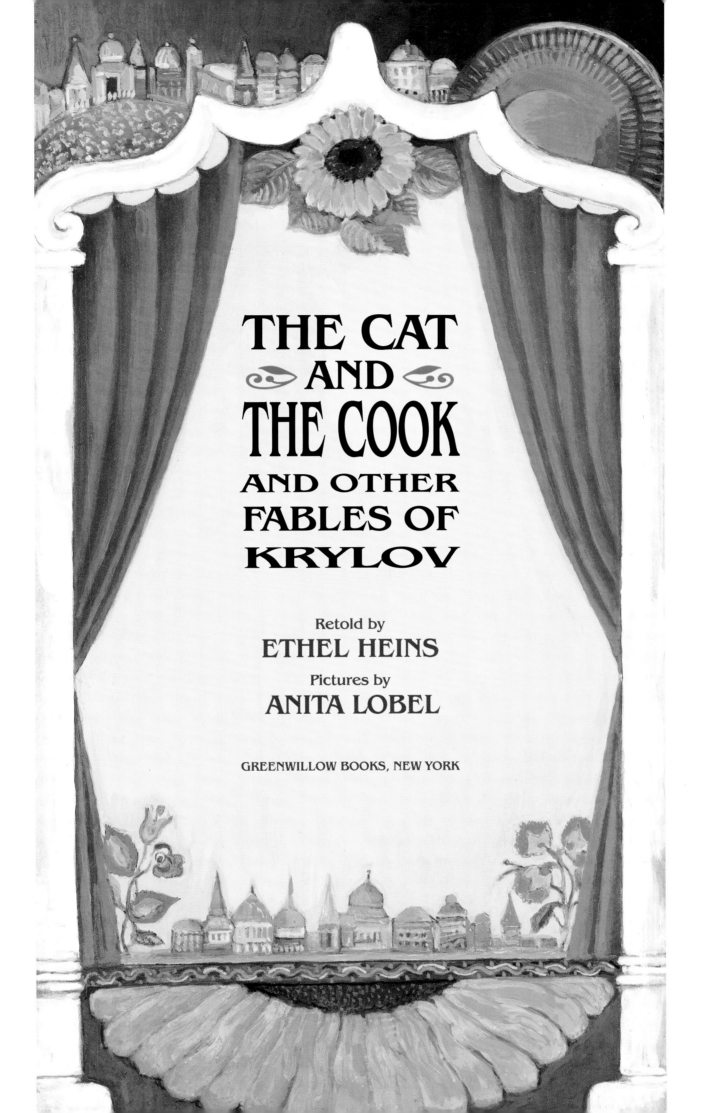

THE CAT
AND
THE COOK
AND OTHER
FABLES OF
KRYLOV

Retold by
ETHEL HEINS

Pictures by
ANITA LOBEL

GREENWILLOW BOOKS, NEW YORK

For Paul

Watercolor and gouache paints were used for the full-color art.
The text type is Palatino.
Text copyright © 1995 by Ethel L. Heins
Illustrations copyright © 1995 by Anita Lobel
All rights reserved. No part of this book may be reproduced or
utilized in any form or by any means, electronic or mechanical,
including photocopying, recording, or by any information
storage and retrieval system, without permission in writing from
the Publisher, Greenwillow Books, a division of William Morrow &
Company, Inc., 1350 Avenue of the Americas, New York, NY 10019.
Printed in Singapore by Tien Wah Press
First Edition 10 9 8 7 6 5 4 3 2 1

Library of Congress Cataloging-in-Publication Data
Heins, Ethel L.
The cat and the cook and other fables of Krylov /
retold by Ethel L. Heins ; pictures by Anita Lobel.
p.   cm.
Includes bibliographical references.
Contents: The kitten and the starling—Fortune and the beggar—
The swan, the pike, and the crab—The eagle and the spider—
The cat and the cook—The quartet—The miser—
The titmouse—The donkey and the bell—
The eagle and the mole—The wolf and the cat—The kite.
ISBN 0-688-12310-4 (trade).   ISBN 0-688-12311-2 (lib. bdg.)
1. Fables, Russian—Translations into English.
2. Children's stories, Russian—Translations into English.
[1. Fables. 2. Short stories.]   I. Lobel, Anita, ill.
II. Krylov, Ivan Andreevich, 1768–1844. Basni.
Selections. 1994.   III. Title.
PZ8.2.H42Cat   1995   [E]—dc20
94-4116   CIP   AC

Contents

The Kitten and the Starling 6

Fortune and the Beggar 8

The Swan, the Pike, and the Crab 11

The Eagle and the Spider 13

The Cat and the Cook 15

The Quartet 17

The Miser 18

The Titmouse 21

The Donkey and the Bell 22

The Eagle and the Mole 24

The Wolf and the Cat 26

The Kite 28

AUTHOR'S NOTE 30

SOURCES 32

The Kitten and the Starling

I n a certain house a kitten once lived companionably with a starling who was kept in a cage. Now, starlings are not the sweetest of singers, but this one was a wise and crafty bird, while the kitten was quiet and mild in manner.

One day it happened that the kitten wasn't fed. Plaintively meowing and gently flicking her tail, she wandered sadly about the house.

"My friend," said the starling, "you're a simpleton to go hungry. Look, right under your nose there's a goldfinch in a cage."

"Oh, no!" responded the kitten. "I couldn't do what you're suggesting—my conscience wouldn't let me."

"What nonsense you talk!" retorted the starling. "You have no idea what the world is like. Only a fool worries about her conscience. Strength, not weakness, is what really counts, and I can easily show you why." And he gave the kitten a lecture to prove his point.

The starling's philosophy convinced the hungry young cat. Seizing the little goldfinch, she swallowed it, but the dainty morsel only sharpened her appetite. So she said to the starling, "Thank you, my kind friend, for the lesson you have taught me." And breaking into the starling's cage, she gobbled up her teacher.

Fortune and the Beggar

A miserable beggar, grumbling at his hard luck, carried a ragged old sack and trudged from house to house. He wondered why wealthy people, in spite of all their luxuries, were seldom content. Craving more and more riches, they often lost their money in foolish ventures.

"Here's a handsome house," the beggar said to himself. "It once belonged to an old merchant who became enormously rich. But no one could persuade him to stop working and spend the rest of his life in peace. Still hungry for gold, he sent out his trading ships once again, but they were wrecked in a storm, and all his treasure went to the bottom of the sea. Another man tried his hand at gambling and quickly made a million, only to lose it in the end. And it served him right; greedy people are never satisfied."

At that moment Dame Fortune suddenly appeared and said to the beggar, "Listen, I'd like to help you. Here are some gold coins I found. Hold out your bag, and I'll fill it—on one condition. Whatever remains in your bag will be pure gold, but whatever spills onto the ground will turn to dust. Be careful. I've warned you, and I shall keep my word. Your bag is worn and threadbare, so don't overload it."

Hardly believing his ears, the beggar was breathless with joy. Opening his sack, he watched as a stream of golden coins poured into it. Soon the sack grew heavy.

"Is it full enough?" asked Dame Fortune.

"No, no, not yet," answered the beggar.

"Is it tearing? I see a hole."

"Don't be afraid. My sack can hold a bit more. Another handful of gold, I beg you."

"That's enough, man! Your bag is going to split!"

"Just a little more. Please."

But at that very moment the sack burst open. The wondrous treasure was strewn over the ground and instantly turned to dust.

Dame Fortune vanished. And the beggar, sighing deeply, went on his way, as poor as ever.

The Swan, the Pike, and the Crab

When partners cannot work together, their project will surely fail.

One day a swan, a pike, and a crab decided to pull a wooden cart. After harnessing themselves together, they tugged and shoved, sweated and strained, but the cart stubbornly refused to budge. The load wasn't very heavy. What was wrong?

Each one was only following his own nature. The swan rose upward in flight, the pike pulled toward a pond, and the crab scuttled backward. So, to this day, the cart still stands where it was.

The Eagle and the Spider

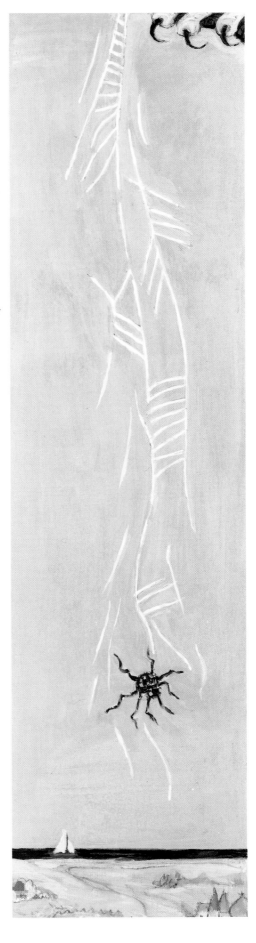

High above the clouds an eagle flew and alighted on a lofty mountain peak. Perched on an ancient tree, he admired the broad landscape below, which seemed to stretch to the very ends of the earth. He saw woods and meadows in the first bloom of spring, sparkling rivers meandering through the plains, and on the horizon the sea, dark as a raven's wing.

The eagle called to the king of the gods, "Praise to you, for giving me such wondrous power that no heights are beyond my reach. I alone can survey all the beauties of the world, for no one has ever flown so high."

"Good heavens! What a boaster you are!" said a small voice. "I dispute your claim. As you can see, here I am, just as high as you are."

The eagle looked down and saw a spider on a nearby branch, busily weaving a silken web as though he were trying to hide the sun from the eagle.

"How did you ever come up to this mountaintop?" asked the eagle. "Even great birds with mighty wings wouldn't attempt such a tremendous flight. You are weak and have no wings at all. Surely you didn't crawl up here, did you?"

"Oh, I could never do that!"

"Then, tell me, how did you get here?"

"Well, I simply attached myself by a thread to your tail feathers—and you brought me up here yourself! But now I can stay without your help, so stop your bragging, please, and don't put on such airs. For remember that I—"

But here a sudden gust of wind caught the conceited spider and whirled him down, down, into the valley far below.

The Cat and the Cook

O nce there was a cook who was much better educated than his fellows. He was able to read and write, and he had a clever way with words. One evening he left his kitchen to join some friends at a nearby tavern. As he had a goodly supply of food, he left his cat to keep it safe from mice and rats.

When he returned, however, he was horrified to see the remains of a pie strewn over the floor. The cat was crouched in a corner, purring contentedly, with a chicken in his mouth.

"Oh, you glutton!" scolded the furious cook. "How dare you face me? Until now you were a trustworthy cat, a model of behavior, who guarded my kitchen faithfully."

The cat, meanwhile, was busily eating the chicken.

"What a disgrace you are!" continued the cook. "Now the neighbors will say, 'That cat is a thief, a criminal! Letting him into the kitchen is like turning a hungry wolf loose in a barnyard.'"

The cat listened but kept right on eating. The cook, however, was determined to preach and teach. He continued to reproach the cat, never stopping the flow of his angry words. Nor did he notice that while he delivered his lecture, the cat calmly finished off the chicken. The cook, it seems, had never learned that words are wasted when it's time for action.

The Quartet

A mischievous monkey, a goat, a donkey, and a great clumsy bear decided to get together and play a quartet. They found sheets of music and gathered some instruments—two fiddles, a cello, and a double bass. Under a tree they sat on the grass and prepared to impress everyone with their performance. Briskly they scratched and scraped the strings and made a fearful noise—but it wasn't music.

"Stop, friends, stop!" cried the monkey. "We can't make music seated this way—it's all wrong. Listen, Bear, take your double bass and sit facing Donkey and his cello. I'll play first fiddle opposite Goat, who will play second fiddle. Then, you'll see, the hills and forests will soon echo with our lovely tunes."

So the four friends changed places, and the quartet began again, but the racket was as deafening as ever.

"Wait a moment!" brayed the donkey. "I know the secret. We must sit side by side, in a row."

Now the animals followed the donkey's advice, and once again everyone changed places. But they sounded no more melodious than before. So the four players began to argue and squabble over where they should sit—and why.

Hearing the noisy quarrel, a nightingale came flying to them.

"Your music is always enchanting," said the monkey. "Please help us with ours," he begged. "Look, we have the notes and the instruments. Just tell us how we should sit."

The nightingale replied patiently, "To make music, you must have talent and skill. It really doesn't matter where you sit. Forgive me, but you will never be musicians."

The Miser

In days long ago, goblins often lived hidden away in houses, carefully guarding them for the human owners.

There was once such a goblin who possessed a treasure, which he kept buried underground. Suddenly the king of the goblins ordered him to a far-distant place, where he was to serve for many years. Like it or not, the goblin was forced to carry out the order.

One problem, however, worried him greatly. Who would keep his treasure safe? He could not hire anyone; that would cost too much. He couldn't leave it buried; a thief might dig it up and steal it. The goblin was puzzled, but at last he had an idea.

The master of the house was a notorious miser. The goblin dug up the treasure and went to the man, saying, "Dear master, I have troubling news. I must leave you and go far away to the other side of the world. I've always been happy here, so I want to give you my gold as a token of friendship. Spend this money as you wish. There is only one condition—that when you die, I alone will be your heir. Meanwhile, may you have good health and a long life." He spoke and was gone.

Twenty years passed, and the goblin's service was finally completed. Wasting no time, he returned home gratefully. To his surprise, he found his master, dead of hunger, stretched across the treasure chest with the key in his hand and all the money safe and sound.

So the goblin had his riches once again and rejoiced in the fact that protecting it had not cost him a penny. "What better person could I have trusted with my gold," he exclaimed, "than a man too stingy to pay for his own food!"

The Titmouse

A titmouse flew to the ocean and declared that he planned to set it on fire. Quickly the astonishing news spread far and wide, arousing both curiosity and fear. The sea creatures were terrified, flocks of birds gathered, and from the forest the animals rushed to the shore to watch the ocean burn. From distant cities greedy folks arrived, ready with spoons to enjoy a steaming fish soup fit for the table of a millionaire.

With wide eyes the crowd gazed at the sea, waiting silently for the miracle. Now and then a whisper was heard. "Look, it's beginning to steam. It will be blazing in a moment." But there was no sign of burning; the ocean neither boiled nor bubbled and, in fact, it never even grew hot.

What happened, in the end, to the silly titmouse? Covered with shame, the little bird flew home to his nest. Would he ever again boast of a deed before it was done?

The Donkey and the Bell

A peasant once owned a gentle, hard-working donkey. His master couldn't praise him too highly. One day, afraid that his donkey might get lost in the woods, the man tied a bell around the animal's neck.

The bell jingled pleasantly as the donkey moved about, and he became quite puffed up with pride. The animal felt as though he were wearing a decoration for good behavior and decided that he must be a very fine creature indeed. But his new importance brought him nothing but trouble—and this can happen to anybody, not only to a donkey!

Before the donkey wore a bell, no one paid much attention to him. He would happily raid a vegetable garden or a field of oats. Then, after he feasted well, he would quietly go home.

But now it was a different story. Wherever the famous donkey appeared, the bell signaled his arrival. The farmers heard the jingle-jangle and came after him. They thrashed him with heavy sticks and drove him away. Thus the unfortunate beast grew weak with hunger until all that remained of him was skin and bones.

The Eagle and the Mole

A mighty eagle and his mate flew to the depths of a forest, far from the world of humans. Choosing a giant oak, they began to build their nest on the topmost branch and to wait for a brood of fledglings.

A tiny mole burrowing in the earth bravely called up to the eagle. "This tree isn't safe for a nest," he said. "The roots are nearly rotted through, and it's ready to topple over."

"Really!" said the eagle to himself. "Am I to take advice from a little mole in a hole? Doesn't he know that the eagle's eye is the sharpest in the world? How dare he meddle in the affairs of the king of birds?"

So the eagle ignored the warning and finished building the nest. All went well, and soon some fine young eagle chicks were added to the family.

One morning at sunrise the proud father flew home to the nest, carrying a tasty breakfast for his brood. But what a terrible sight met his eyes! The oak tree had crashed to the ground and lay shattered; his mate and her young had perished.

In his sorrow the great eagle cried out, "I've been punished because I was too proud to listen to a mole's warning. But how should I know that such an insignificant creature might be wise enough to give advice to an eagle?"

A small voice answered. "You should not have scorned me," the mole said. "Remember that I live in an underground home. Nobody knows better than I whether or not the roots of a tree are healthy and strong."

The Wolf and the Cat

Out of the forest and into the village dashed a wolf—not to kill but to save his own skin. A group of hunters and a pack of hounds were pursuing him, and he feared for his life. In vain he sought shelter, for every gate was latched.

At that moment the wolf noticed a cat perched on a fence. "Tell me, friend puss," gasped the wolf, "is there a kind peasant around here who would save me from my enemies? Just listen to those hunting horns and the yelping of the dogs!"

The cat answered, "Hurry and find Stephen—there's no better man."

"That's true," said the wolf, trembling with fear, "but he knows I recently stole one of his sheep."

"Well, then, try Damien."

"Oh, he's angry with me, too. I carried off one of his goats."

"Then turn in right here. Ivan may help you."

"Ivan? I wouldn't dare meet up with him! He's been looking for me ever since I took a lamb from his pasture last spring."

"Oh, dear," said the cat, "you really are in trouble. The only other one I can suggest is Michael. Maybe you'll have some luck with him."

"Michael—never!" cried the wolf. "He'd be after me with a gun. I killed one of his young calves and ate it."

"Well, my friend," concluded the cat, "you won't find mercy in any corner of this village. What do you expect? No peasant is stupid enough to protect a killer. You have no one to blame but yourself."

The Kite

A paper kite, tossed about by the wind, soared high over the hills toward the sky. Observing a butterfly far below, the kite called out, "You foolish little thing, I can hardly see you trying to fly way down there. It must make you jealous to look at me."

"Oh, no! Not at all," replied the butterfly. "I don't envy you. Yes, you fly high, but don't forget that you are tied fast to a string for someone else's amusement. It's true that I cannot hope to reach your great heights. But I roam where I wish. I am free."

Author's Note

Ivan Andreevich Krylov, Russia's great fabulist, was born in 1768, the son of a minor army officer. After the death of his father, his mother moved to St. Petersburg in order to obtain a widow's pension, for she was determined that the boy receive a respectable education. Ivan became a voracious reader and at fourteen secured a job as a clerk in the civil service.

Before long he launched his literary career by writing the text for a comic opera. He continued to produce other works for the theater, at the same time writing for a variety of short-lived magazines. Dabbling also in music and painting, Ivan soon moved easily in artistic and literary circles. Always fascinated by the racy speech of Russian peasants, he began to collect a rich store of the terse, idiomatic language he was to use in his fables.

Not until Krylov was nearly forty did he realize where his creative power lay. His early fables were merely adaptations, chiefly from La Fontaine. But he eventually abandoned this dependence and struck off on his own, writing over 150 vigorous original fables full of wit and wisdom and cast in polished metrical form. From the beginning they were eagerly snatched up by editors of literary journals; Krylov's initial collection was published in 1809, achieving a success unprecedented in Russia. For the rest of his life the poet wrote nothing but fables.

By nature Krylov was lazy, untidy, and pleasantly eccentric. In 1812 he was appointed to a congenial position in the St. Petersburg Imperial Public Library. Here he had his own comfortable living quarters, and for the next thirty years he lived a quiet, carefree life. Meanwhile his volumes of fables became Russia's first best-sellers; his contemporary, Alexander Pushkin, called him "the most national and most popular of our poets."

The appeal of Krylov's fables to children was instantaneous, and succeeding generations of Russians have been brought up on them. When the poet died in 1844, children from all over the country contributed to a fund for a memorial. A bronze statue was erected in the Summer Garden in St. Petersburg. There he still sits, an open book in his hand; the pedestal is decorated with the figures of animals that appear in the fables. To this day children can be found playing on the sandy ground that surrounds the monument.

Translating Krylov's fables into English verse has been a challenging exercise for linguistic scholars. But in order to convey the essential narratives to children, I rendered the stilted translations into storytelling prose. Although I have tried to remain faithful to the spirit of the poet's original fables, I am aware that my retellings cannot do full justice to his intensely Russian expression.

Sources

Krylov, Ivan A. *Kriloff's Fables*, translated from the Russian into English in the original metres by C. Fillingham Coxwell. London: Kegan Paul, Trench, Trubner & Co., and New York: E. P. Dutton Co., n.d. [1920].

Krylov, Ivan A. *Kriloff's Original Fables*, translated by I. Henry Harrison. London: Remington & Co., 1883.

Krylov, Ivan A. *Russian Fables of Ivan Krylov*, with verse translation by Bernard Pares. Harmondsworth, England, and New York: Penguin, 1942. (Reprinted from *Krylov's Fables*, translated into English verse with a preface by Barnard Pares. New York: Harcourt, Brace, 1927.)

Krylov, Ivan A. *Krilof and His Fables*, by W. R. S. Ralston. London: Strahan and Co., 1869.